HEAVY FREIGHT

Sigmund Brouwer

orca soundings

ORCA BOOK PUBLISHERS

Library and Archives Canada Cataloguing in Publication

Brouwer, Sigmund, 1959-, author
Heavy freight / Sigmund Brouwer.
(Orca soundings)

Issued in print and electronic formats.
ISBN 978-1-4598-1475-2 (softcover).—ISBN 978-1-4598-1476-9 (pdf).—
ISBN 978-1-4598-1477-6 (epub)

I. Title. II. Series: Orca soundings
PS8553.R68467H43 2017   jC813'.54   C2017-900872-2
C2017-900873-0

First published in the United States, 2017
Library of Congress Control Number: 2017933025

Summary: In this high-interest novel for teen readers, Max Stone hops on a
freight train to seek out the dad who abandoned him when he was a baby.

*Orca Book Publishers is dedicated to preserving the environment and has
printed this book on Forest Stewardship Council® certified paper.*

Orca Book Publishers gratefully acknowledges the support for its
publishing programs provided by the following agencies: the Government
of Canada through the Canada Book Fund and the Canada Council
for the Arts, and the Province of British Columbia through
the BC Arts Council and the Book Publishing Tax Credit.

Editor: Tanya Trafford
Cover image by Getty Images

ORCA BOOK PUBLISHERS
www.orcabook.com

Printed and bound in Canada.

20 19 18 17 • 4 3 2 1

To Adam Hucal. You rock!

Chapter One

Seriously? Stone thought. Dog? Already?

It was a massive German shep-
herd in a K-9 vest, closing in fast on
him, so near that Stone could hear its
claws clicking on the pavement. Not yet
midnight, and already Stone's night was
about to end.

So much to hate about dog.

Cop in car—no problem. Here on East Hastings, Maxwell Stone knew every inch of alley, every cubbyhole. Headlights and searchlights gave easy warning of any Vancouver Police Department patrol-car approach and lots of time to duck out of sight.

Cop on foot—laughable. Stone was fifteen, looked thirteen. What was a cop going to do, shoot him in the back? Let some lucky bystander scoop it on video and cash in on thirty seconds of YouTube fame?

Second advantage to Stone in the ongoing game called Stone versus VPD were his soft-soled Nikes, a couple of ounces of foam and nylon with air-cushioned soles. Well worth the shoplifting risk. Cops had clunkers for shoes. Cops had belts that weighted them down with flashlight, pistol, mace, handcuffs, radio. Stone ran with Olympic-level speed compared to a cop. Even if he couldn't lose them on a stretch, he cornered better, a gazelle compared to a rhino.

Stone remembered the winter before, when a cop had skidded on cobblestone on a sharp turn from sidewalk into alley and gone butt sideways, thumping into a snowbank. Stone had stopped, snapped a shot from his smartphone, then posted it later on a social-media account that didn't belong to him. Enjoyed watching it go viral. He'd made sure to email it to the public-relations dork for VPD too. With a message. *Here's one of your men in blue looking like a drunk Frosty the Snowman.*

Cop anytime.

But dog?

That was low. Nasty. Dog you couldn't bluff. Dog couldn't be fooled by lies. Dog couldn't be distracted by five-dollar bills tossed in the air, giving Stone the little head start he needed to escape any human.

Dog was all teeth and blurred legs. And nose. Dog was nose, better than any kind of thermal imaging in the abandoned buildings Stone had roamed since he was a kid.

Five minutes earlier Stone had been doing a simple business transaction with some dude from an out-of-district preppy high school. Bottle of pills for a handful of cash. Preppy Dude had decided that nine inches of height on Stone and having his girlfriend as spectator earned him the right to play tough guy.

Preppy Dude had taken the pills, then sneered and pulled out a knife. Pills in one hand and knife in the other, Preppy Dude had then asked if Stone had a problem with just walking away without any holes in his skin. And without cash.

Stone's response?

Stone had gagged as if terrified, then wiped a hand across his mouth.

Then he'd retched and hurled a hot stream of vomit all over Preppy Dude's chest and knife hand. Normally, Stone didn't shoot vomit at people, but come on—the dude had pulled a knife.

Stone's aim had been perfect, the stream even splattering Preppy Dude's face. Preppy Dude had dropped the knife, shrieked and wiped at his eyes. Shrieked. Yeah. Like a five-year-old girl.

Stone had taken advantage of Preppy Dude's shock, grabbing the knife and snatching back his bottle of pills.

That's when a cruising patrol car had turned into the alley, headlights catching the three of them in a brief frozen pose. Stone with knife in hand, girlfriend with her hands covering her mouth in horror and Preppy Dude flailing around as if Stone had stabbed him.

Not a chance the cop would take Stone's word over the other two's. Stone had dropped the knife—but not the pills—and bolted, not too worried about the cop actually catching him.

Then dog had appeared. Must have been a K-9 unit in the back of the car. Maybe it had been a training run. The explanation didn't really matter.

Stone was on the run. With dog in pursuit.

He'd heard plenty of stories about dog. Like when VPD handlers were in a bad mood, they gave the attack command instead of the takedown command. Last thing you wanted was a K-9 dragging you down by your privates. Winning a million-dollar lawsuit didn't matter. much if getting neutered was the price you paid for it.

Dog. In pursuit.

It was a sprinting bullet of a shadow with deadly and silent intent, focused only on Stone.

Chapter Two

Ahead of him, parked in the darkness of a narrow alley, Stone spotted a
painter's van. He could just make out
the aluminum ladder strapped to the
roof, overhanging it by a couple of feet
front and back.

Perfect.

With the dog unleashed and way
ahead of the handler, all Stone needed

was a moment out of reach of the dog. Maybe two.

He stayed at full sprint, reaching the van just ahead of the dog.

Stone judged it perfectly. First step on the front bumper, left hand reaching for the base of the antenna near the windshield on the passenger side. He let momentum carry him up the slanted hood, left hand pulling on the antenna to keep him from sliding off, then right hand reaching high to grab the end of the ladder that extended over the roof.

It felt smooth. Left hand releasing the antenna to grab the ladder too. Feet still moving in a fast crab walk up the windshield. Body briefly almost horizontal. Final throw of the feet and a twist that put his hip onto the top part of the ladder. A grunt to slide his body fully on top of the ladder and just like that, he was on top of the van's roof, ladder between him and the dog.

Not a heartbeat too soon.

The dog had leaped, but its jaws snapped on one of Stone's back pockets. There was the sound of ripping fabric, but Stone was safe. The dog slid down the hood of the van.

Stone scrambled to his feet on the roof of the van, legs straddling the ladder. The dog circled the van, whining in frustration.

All Stone had to do now was figure out how to loosen the ladder from the bungee straps that held it to the van roof and then prop it against the apartment balcony just above the van. Quick climb there would lead him to the fire-escape stairs, and before the cops arrived, he'd be on the roof. From there, if he couldn't figure out a way to escape he deserved to have his butt thrown in jail.

Even so, he and his butt would be all in one piece. No dog dragging him down until the handcuffs arrived.

Then he heard a deep voice. It came from the open window of the passenger side of the van.

"Hello, young man. What exactly are you doing up there?"

Okay, the question didn't sound exactly like that. It started with words that didn't belong in church, ended with words that didn't belong in church, and in the middle questioned Stone's sanity in an equally aggressive way.

"I'm a tad occupied here," Stone said, thinking it was great that someone was inside the van. It meant that now he didn't need to do anything about the ladder. All he had to do was mention the police. To disguise his voice, he snapped back in a perfect British accent, the one he had practiced from watching YouTube videos.

Not posh. This wasn't the time or place to be posh. This was a time to be snarling, street-weary tough. "Go back to picking your nits. The filth will be here soon enough to haul you away."

"Filth?" the guy asked.

"Coppers, you div."

Stone figured that would do it. Dudes parked in a van late at night probably didn't want to encourage a police visit. Not around here. The Downtown Eastside, or DTES—a couple dozen square blocks along East Hastings, between Main Street and Cambie—was one of Vancouver's sketchiest areas. For Stone, kindergarten had not been about the ABCs. Instead he'd learned not to touch needles left behind by druggies. He'd learned to be okay with food from dumpsters. And he'd learned to read body language, because not reading body language meant getting robbed or beaten.

Then he'd learned how to take care of his mom. Because she didn't seem to be good at learning those lessons.

"Hey." Another voice, coming from the driver's side. "It's that British kid. He let the air out of my tires last month."

Uh-oh. Stone had assumed the van dudes were here to make a deal. Had thought he'd be better off disguising his voice. Instead, turned out they were locals. Now he'd have to watch out for them for months.

But first he needed to stay out of reach of the K-9, which was still whining at the side of the van. He'd give himself the luxury of worrying about these guys later. Which meant that since they already knew who he was, it couldn't be any worse to get them really mad.

"Isn't this some hard cheese?" Stone said. "You being the shitehawk down there and me all cozy and safe up here till the filth arrives to rescue me from you and your guns."

"No guns here. We're not idiots."

Stone said, "That's not what they'll hear from me, you manky git."

"Gonna rip out that tongue of yours," the voice said.

Stone laughed. He knew the dog was now protection of sorts. "Fine with me, mate."

The van door began to open. The police dog made a scramble to the sound. The door slammed shut again, and another couple of f-bombs drifted out from both windows.

Yeah. The dog was great protection. Ironic in a delicious way.

Stone turned his attention back to the ladder. It was just held in place by bungee cords. Easy enough to release, if he needed to. But he wouldn't need to.

Not a chance the two in the van would want to be around when the VPD arrived.

The van's engine started.

Exactly what Stone had expected. He grinned. Nothing like a plan falling into place.

Chapter Three

What Stone didn't expect, a hundred yards down the road with the K-9 chasing the van enthusiastically but losing ground, was a hard slam on the brakes. If he hadn't been belly down on top of the ladder, holding on with both hands and enjoying the breeze on his face, the sudden deceleration would have tossed him onto the pavement.

They were on Columbia Street, a one-way headed north of the much busier East Hastings. No traffic here this late at night. No one around to interfere, not that the residents of the DTES were in the habit of getting involved.

Stone admired the brilliance of the move. Had he been thrown to the pavement, Van Dudes would have been able to grab him while he was still dazed, throw him in the van and then who knows what. He'd have been lucky not to be beaten to death. He'd managed to keep his grip though.

Seconds later the van beneath him took off hard. The K-9 was in hard pursuit, moving from streetlight to streetlight at a full run. Stone guessed Van Dudes would try it again, the quick-stop thing. Columbia ended in a T-intersection, and they'd have enough speed by then to make it really hard for Stone to hold on.

Stone rolled off the ladder, keeping one hand on a roof bar that ran along one side of the van. With his other hand, he flipped off one end of the bungee cord holding the ladder in place at the front.

Next was the dangerous part. He needed to turn his entire body to reach the bungee cord at the rear. If the driver slammed on the brakes while Stone was vulnerable, he'd be a Stone in a slingshot, about to eat pavement. But they were still trying to gather speed, and Stone was able to reverse his body in the few seconds it took the van to accelerate, keeping one hand on the roof bar. With his other hand, he flipped off the end of the second bungee cord.

And grinned again. Escape was always a major rush.

Stone wished he could witness what would happen the next time they hit the brakes. But he would be otherwise occupied. Facing the rear, he clutched the roof bar with both hands and watched the gap between him and the chasing K-9 grow to a safe distance. The plan was, as soon as they braked, the ladder would slide past him and over the hood of the van. As the ladder tumbled down onto the road and forced the van to come to a complete stop, he'd scramble down the back of the van and cut through an alley, well clear of the K-9.

Except it turned out a bit differently than Stone imagined.

Yes, the quick stop put some major g-force on his hands. Yes, he managed to hold on. Yes, the ladder tumbled forward and clattered onto the pavement. Yes, the van came to a complete halt just short of the ladder. Yes, he scrambled down the back of the van. Yes, he had enough distance from the K-9 to make his escape.

But what he hadn't considered was that Van Dudes would leave their doors open as they both hopped out and made a dash toward the ladder. Or that the driver would leave the engine running.

Okay, new plan.

Instead of darting into an alley, he spun around to the driver's side and slipped in behind the steering wheel. He reached across, grabbed the handle of the passenger door and slammed it shut. Slammed the driver's door shut. Hit the electric lock. And there he was, safely behind glass and steel with the morons on the other side, screaming at him, pounding on the windows.

Stone smiled at both of them while he casually slipped the seat belt over his shoulders and clicked it into place. As soon as the morons realized what that meant, they screamed louder.

Oh yeah, Stone thought, this is going to be fun. After all, Van Dudes were already insane with anger. Stealing their van wouldn't make much of a difference at this point.

Stone hadn't driven a vehicle before, but he had been a passenger plenty of times. So he knew enough to hit the brake before shifting into Drive. Hands on the steering wheel. Gas pedal next.

Stone looked up to see one of the Van Dudes in the van's headlights. He tried hitting the brakes. Not soon enough. The van banged into Van Dude, flipping him backward. Stone could hear screams of pain through the closed windows.

Stone knew he was dead if they ever caught up to him. And he knew they wouldn't stop hunting him, not ever.

The other Van Dude was banging on the side of the van, the K-9 was still chasing hard, and somewhere behind that was a VPD cop in a patrol car.

Stone needed to be gone. Now.

He smashed the gas pedal against the floor again, and the van thundered ahead. Ladder was in the way on the pavement in front of him, but that wasn't a problem. He drove right over it, enjoying the sound of screeching metal and the thumps along the bottom of the van.

But then something went wrong with the front tire, and the steering wheel suddenly jerked hard to the right.

He spun the steering wheel the other way and tried to hit the brakes. He hit the gas pedal instead. The van lurched hard left, picking up speed. He spun to the right again, concentrating so hard on keeping the van going straight between rows of parked cars that he left his foot on the gas pedal.

Other pedal! Other pedal!

Stone found the brake with his left foot and put his full weight on it. But hadn't taken his right foot off the gas. The van weaved hard, engine screaming, brakes screaming.

He realized his mistake. Took the foot off the gas.

Tires screeched as the van starting slewing sideways with the brakes shuddering the vehicle. Stone spun the steering wheel again. He almost managed to bring the van to a stop as a parked car loomed in front of him. Almost.

Bang!

The van smashed into the parked car, sending it sideways. Airbags deployed. Fabric scraped his face. He choked on the powder that was released when the airbag exploded.

Half blind, he fumbled for the seatbelt release. He found it, slipped the door open and landed on his feet on the street.

The situation hadn't changed. Van Dude One probably needed an ambulance, Van Dude Two was closing in, the K-9 was gaining, and the cops would be here way too soon.

Stone did the only thing he could do. Did what he always did and felt born to do.

He ran.

Chapter Four

Strange, Stone thought, how a person felt most alive when in danger. Maybe that was why he always pushed things, putting himself in situations where if he made the wrong split-second choice, he wouldn't have a chance to make another.

His legs churned, but with his body in full motion, his brain floated calmly above it all as he made a series of snap decisions.

T-intersection ahead where Columbia hit Alexander.

Left turn or right?

Neither.

Straight across to the sidewalk that ran along the train tracks.

No entry to the train yard. Chain-link fence with barbed wire ran along the tracks. Except for the spot just left of the Columbia Pumping Station, a long, narrow brick building that backed onto the train tracks.

There the fence was decorative. No chain link. No barbed wire.

Jump the fence, zip across the tracks.

But if he could jump it, so could the K-9.

Except on the other side of the fence, a freight train was just starting to roll, headed inland.

Sigmund Brouwer

That was it then.

Run hard.

Jump the fence.

Run hard.

Run hard.

Cut across just in front of the train, beat the dog by enough steps that the moving train blocks the dog.

Then slow to a jog to East Waterfront Road on the other side of the tracks.

Disappear.

Lots of places to escape along the waterfront.

Stone pictured it all happening, in beautiful slow motion across his imagination. This train yard was the last stop, the most western point in Canada. Dozens of docks and wharves filled the shoreline. Ships came in full, dropped off freight. Trains took the freight east, through the mountains, to the rest of Canada. Even an idiot could find a spot to hide in that kind of chaos and confusion.

Yeah. His brain floated. Still calm. The plan would work.

Stone found a burst of energy. The soles of his Nikes slapped staccato against the pavement as he crossed Alexander and reached the train yard. Filled with adrenaline, he didn't even feel the effort of scaling the fence.

He was in the train yard, dozens of tracks ahead of him to cross.

The train rumbled in the darkness of the yard, slowly picking up speed. Still time to cut in front of it.

Five steps into the train yard his plan went wrong.

The tracks weren't flat pavement. The tracks were chunks of buried lumber holding steel rail in place. Gravel filled the gaps between the lumber. No way to maintain his pace. A flat-out sprint would guarantee a snapped ankle. Especially in these shadows.

Streetlights gave him enough illumination to confirm the worst. He'd reach the train *after* the front engine passed. He'd be blocked the way he'd expected the dog would be blocked—on the same side of the train as the dog.

A quick glance showed him that the K-9 had cleared the fence. Four legs, not two. Easier for the dog to run across the lumber and gravel and tracks.

Stone refused to stop running. Refused to panic. There was always another way.

He grinned.

Yeah. Always another way.

The front three engines had already passed, and the first ten cars of the chain behind it were boxcars. Sliding doors on their sides. Fifth car down showed a black vertical stripe, the gap of a door open just wide enough for Stone to fit inside.

Ten steps more, pushing as hard as he dared, his feet coming down awkwardly.

He reached the train and ran alongside, expecting it to be easy to keep pace.

But the train was picking up speed.

It was going to take his last burst of energy.

He sprinted. Jumped. Grabbed for one of the bars at the side door. One hand made solid contact. The other hand fell away.

But he couldn't let go.

Huge rolling wheels just behind him. Too much danger of a leg getting caught between wheels and track. Not able to claw his way up with one hand.

All he could do was hang on as his body tumbled beneath him.

He could feel his hand losing grip. He was going to fall. If he couldn't find a way to push his body from the rails beneath him, he would lose a leg. Maybe both. Then bleed out.

Stone realized he was wrong. Sometimes you got to a point where there *wasn't* another way. For the first time in his life, he'd reached it.

Stone screamed. Not fear. In anger.

But then, just as his fingers slipped, a huge arm reached out from inside the car. A hand clamped onto his wrist. He felt like a puppet, yanked upward and inward. The darkness of the boxcar closed him in from the rest of the world, and the train rumbled away from East Hastings.

Chapter Five

When the train stopped hours later, the sky was still dark. Lights down the track gave some illumination inside the boxcar, enough to show that Train Dude hadn't moved from the place he had been when Stone drifted into sleep, bunching his lightweight summer jacket into a pillow. The jacket was red on the outside but tan on the inside. It was a reversible. Stone liked that. It made it seem like he had two jackets, not one.

Stone had woken because the sound of the rumbling had changed and then finally ended. He had no idea what time it was. Like, who wore a watch when you had a smartphone? Except he no longer had it. It had been in his back pocket. It must have fallen out when that stupid K-9 lunged up at him. Meant it was probably lying on the pavement near where he'd first jumped on the van.

No smartphone was bad news. Worse than having no money. Stone could always mooch, steal or dumpster-dive what he needed for food, could always find a doorway to get out of bad weather and sleep for a few hours, could always find a bathroom in a McDonald's to drop a load or use the sink for a bird bath to clean up. After that, all he needed was a smartphone. But with the way they were protected these days with passwords, and tracked with GPS, stealing one was stupid. Good news was, the one he had lost was password protected. So whoever had already scooped it up was basically holding a paperweight and couldn't get at his private information.

Still, losing the smartphone meant losing so many things—camera, Internet, flashlight, music, weather report, movies, Instagram. How humans had survived before the invention of devices was incomprehensible to Stone.

With the train now motionless, Stone was in one corner of the boxcar, Train Dude in the corner diagonally across from Stone. That put as much distance as possible between them.

Keeping their distance had been Stone's choice.

After pulling Stone into the boxcar, Train Dude hadn't said a word. Fifteen minutes of questions from Stone had been met with silence. Train Dude was probably crazy. Stone couldn't jump out of the boxcar—the train had been moving too fast. So choosing the opposite corner made him feel better.

Stone had tried to stay awake, worried that the dude might try something crazy. But after the rush of adrenaline from his escape, his body had crashed. Sure, Stone had a bottle of pills in his pocket, but only losers used drugs. The only type of capsule Stone ever ingested was one with dried mustard powder, and that was only in emergencies.

Sleep had hit Stone hard. He liked sleep. East Hastings didn't exist while he was asleep.

Now he was awake, and the train wasn't moving. He needed to pee, and he was thirsty. His mouth tasted like dirty socks.

The door to the boxcar was open, so all he had to do was hop out and figure out where he was.

Train Dude didn't make a move as Stone edged his way to the door. Stone had made his decision to escape the boxcar, so he didn't hesitate. At the edge of the boxcar he dropped to his butt, feet sticking out. He pushed off and landed lightly on the gravel below.

From inside, a voice deep and low reached him. "Siding. Nowhere to go. Unless you like bears and mosquitoes."

Stone turned back to the boxcar. From where he stood, the floor of the boxcar was level with his chin.

"Siding?" Stone asked.

"Mile marker number—"

"Mile? You American?"

"Someone who knows trains. Canadian railways didn't switch to metric. We're pulled over for an east-bound train to pass. It's called a siding. You want off, Kamloops is the next train yard. Best thing you could do is ride to Kamloops and use that as a jumping-off point."

Looked like the truth. Light came from a single bulb on a stick and a square box. Other than that, it was dark, middle-of-the-wilderness dark.

"So, mate," Stone said, "what's your name?"

Silence answered him from the Train Dude's corner of the boxcar.

"Sweet Fanny Adams," Stone said. British accent had hurt him back in Vancouver, but for disguise here, it was the best he could do. Again, not posh. He needed to sound rough. "It's going to be like that? All chatty on me?"

More silence.

Stone shook his head in disgust. He didn't see much choice but to get back inside the boxcar. Kamloops. How bad could it be? Especially because it would be suicide to return to East Hastings. Cops wouldn't get him. They never did. Cops played by the rules.

The Van Dudes though—they were something else. They'd break the rules and then they'd break Stone. As long as Stone could find a way to make sure his mom was okay back in Vancouver, any place but East Hastings was a good place to be.

Kamloops it was then. But not before taking care of urgent business.

Stone turned away from the boxcar and relieved himself, taking satisfaction in the sound of splatter against gravel.

Then he climbed back up and went to his corner of the boxcar and waited for the train to get moving again.

Chapter Six

For a second time, the changing rhythm of the train's motion brought Stone out of a restless sleep. Brightness against his eyelids told him that dawn had arrived. Caution kept him from opening his eyes and betraying that he was awake. Train Dude was on the other side of the boxcar, and Stone wanted a chance to observe. He hadn't tried anything like robbing Stone, or worse, but that didn't mean it was too late for Train Dude to finally show bad intentions.

Stone rolled over as if it were a natural part of his sleep. He found a position on the rough wood floor of the boxcar in which he could curl his head into his chest and peer through nearly closed eyelids to assess the situation.

He saw daylight from the open boxcar doors. It showed a slowing blur of brown hills dotted by spruce trees. Or pine trees. Stone didn't really care about trees.

It was weird, though, seeing actual hills outlined against a blue sky. His entire life, he'd never been more than twenty blocks in either direction of the East Hastings area of Vancouver. Scenery like this he'd only seen on television or in movies.

As for Train Dude, Stone's limited vision stopped him from satisfying his curiosity, aside from confirming that the man was huge. Big, Stone understood. Just about any adult male was big compared to Stone. But Train Dude had a serious largeness to him, made more menacing by his stillness.

Train Dude wore a black hoodie, and his face was obscured. Black jeans. Black work boots. Beside him was a small black backpack. Maybe the guy didn't know that colors existed in the world.

The backpack squawked.

Squawked?

It was a fuzzy kind of high-pitched noise. Stone wasn't going to ask. He decided he was going to pretend to be asleep until the train stopped, hoping Train Dude would just jump out. Then Stone could go on his way.

The slowing process of the train continued. It was gradual. That made sense to Stone. You couldn't just slam on the brakes and expect a train to stop.

That reminded Stone of the night before, of slamming on the brakes of the van and how it had crashed and the airbags had exploded. Pretty cool, the accident. What was not so cool was knowing Van Dudes would be waiting for any rumors of Stone's presence in the neighborhood.

Stone kept his eyes in the nearly shut position. Through the crack of his lids he saw houses among the trees on the hillsides. Ten minutes later the train reached a full stop.

Train Dude stood and stretched. His face remained hidden in his hoodie. He picked up his backpack and moved to sit at the edge of the boxcar. Without a word, he jumped down and disappeared.

Stone decided to give Train Dude a five-minute head start. Then he'd head out for food. Maybe he could find someone to buy his prescription pills off him.

He tapped the bottle in his front pocket to reassure himself it was still there. The pills gave a comforting rattle.

Stone smiled. He had lots of ways of surviving.

Without a smartphone to mark time, he started counting. He'd give himself five minutes. So five times sixty seconds meant that at the three-hundred mark, it would be safe to bust out himself.

He'd find a McDonald's, then a library, see what he could find online about how bad Van Dude One had been hurt. Stone loved public libraries. Summers, he practically lived at the Carnegie branch of the Vancouver Public Library, the big, beautiful stone building representing the dignity that Stone craved for his own life. His VPL card was in his front pocket, a reminder that less than twenty-four hours earlier, he'd expected no breaks in the routine of his life.

Stone kept counting.

At 221, someone popped his head inside the boxcar and pinned Stone with a flashlight beam.

Chapter Seven

"Need you out of here, duke," a male voice behind the beam said. Stone couldn't see the man's face behind the flashlight. He didn't sound particularly aggressive.

"Clearly," Stone said in a chirpy and cheerful British accent. Now was a time to talk posh. Upper-class and respectable.

"The advice is much appreciated. Ta. I'll be off then."

Stone stood, hoping a shift of movement would give him a chance to see past the flashlight beam, but it stayed in his eyes. Daylight outside. Dark in the boxcar. Visually, it put Stone at a disadvantage.

"Not so fast, duke. You're trespassing in a rail yard."

Duke? Again? Perhaps a reference to his British accent? Stone wondered.

"Don't mean to be a bother," Stone said. He took a step, hoping to be able to jump past flashlight dude. "Ta then."

The beam stayed right in his eyes. Stone had to shield his face with his hand.

"With runaways," Flashlight Dude said, "we check with Vancouver to see if parents have called in a missing person. You got some sort of identification you could show me?"

Last thing Stone wanted was for anyone to search him and find the VPL card on him . It had his full name on it. Not good, especially with someone maybe dead back in Vancouver.

Stone edged toward the open doors, hands in his pockets. "Vancouver? Not my domicile."

Usually his posh accent softened situations. Not here.

"Train came from nowhere else," Flashlight Dude said. "So already I know you like telling lies. Makes me want to find out what other lies you are telling. Interesting job like that really brightens up my day. Why don't you just hop down, and we'll continue this conversation out here. Let's start with you showing me some identification, like I asked."

What if Van Dude One hadn't survived? That was vehicular homicide right there. Stone had to figure a way out of this new mess.

If only he had his device. He would have been able to google whether the VPD was hunting for him. Until he knew for sure, any kind of conversation with authorities was dangerous.

"Happy to oblige," Stone said, palming a homemade pill from the ready stash he always kept in his pocket. He pulled his hands out of his pocket, with the VPL library card visible as if he was going to offer it. "Hang on then."

Stone put up his hand, gesturing for a second or two, and coughed hard. He pretended to cover his mouth and popped the pill into his mouth. But he didn't swallow or chew. It wasn't yet time to release the dried mustard powder that it contained.

Stone reached the edge of the boxcar and slid onto his butt to jump down.

Now he could clearly see Flashlight Dude, who was staying out of arm's reach.

The dude wore a police hat, and his waist belt had all the tools of a cop—pistol, handcuffs, radio, baton. A badge on the shoulder of his navy-blue uniform clearly showed a logo and the phrase CN *Police*.

Parked nearby was a truck—white with two horizontal stripes and a matching police logo.

"Canadian Police then?" Stone asked, speaking around a big gob of spit in his mouth. "The CN stands for Canadian?"

"Canadian National. CN Railway. I'm an officer of the CN Police Service. Now how about handing me your identification."

A train cop then.

"Brilliant," Stone said. He was using conversation to distract the cop.

"And you've been trained in first aid, I hope. I haven't been feeling very well…"

Stone chewed down on the pill, releasing the mustard powder. Two seconds later, he retched. There wasn't much left in his stomach, not after the discharge on Preppy Dude the night before, but there was still enough liquid to burn Stone's throat as it rose. He vomited outward, past Train Cop, and streamed it to the ground.

Train Cop would have been inhuman not to look. That was enough of a distraction for Stone to zip onto the ground and dash hard for the cop's vehicle.

The driver's door was unlocked. Stone had enough of a head start to slide in. Perfect. The keys were in the ignition, with a big clump of other keys on a heavy key chain.

No way was he going to be stupid enough to drive this like he'd done with the van the night before. Moving a cop vehicle even a hundred yards would make it theft, and then they'd look for him forever.

Instead, he locked the driver's-side door as the cop finally recovered and lunged toward the vehicle. The cop pulled uselessly at the door handle.

Stone grabbed the keys from the ignition and slid out the passenger door.

"Don't make this more serious than it is," Train Cop snarled.

"Brilliant idea," Stone said. He was safe with the vehicle between them. "I could have taken your truck, but think of how embarrassing it would be to report that some kid stole your vehicle. So the way I look at it, you owe me one. Ta, then!"

Stone threw the key chain as hard as he could over the boxcar he'd just escaped from.

It clanked somewhere on the other side. He figured it should take the Train Cop at least five minutes to find his keys. Stone bolted. It was what he did best.

Chapter Eight

Stone was hungry, so first things first. He had to find a McDonald's or a Tim Hortons.

Escaping the rail yard had been relatively easy. Train Cop had given up pursuing on foot in the first thirty seconds. Even if he'd used his radio to call for backup, it would have been too late. Just down the tracks, Stone reached an open gate where Train Cop had driven into the rail yard. He jogged out onto a street. This side of the tracks was neatly lined with older homes and yards with mature trees. This was definitely not like the landscape of East Hastings, with rows and rows of apartment buildings and warehouses. The other side of the tracks showed the roofline of commercial buildings. That was more his kind of landscape, so that was his destination. Commercial areas were where people gathered, and where people gathered, he felt comfortable. And invisible.

Instead of going down the road to find a place to cross the tracks to reach those buildings, he dashed in the opposite direction for three blocks. Seemed smart not to do what cops might expect him to do. It took him to a riverbank that ran parallel to the tracks behind him. He ducked behind a tree and peeled off his jacket. He reversed it to show the tan. That was another reason he liked the jacket. Red was a flashy color. Red was what people remembered when he ran away from them. Once he'd escaped, the tan let him blend into crowds.

Stone relaxed now and began to walk. He followed a recreation path along the river, knowing nobody would be able to follow him by vehicle. He walked for about ten minutes, then cut back to the tracks to look for a place to cross over.

Stone was careful to memorize the street signs and made a note that he was on Lorne Street, which ran alongside the tracks.

At Third Ave there was a pedestrian overpass. To Stone, that was an obvious place to get trapped if Train Cop was still looking for him. He kept going.

At Second Ave he could have crossed over. There were only two sets of train tracks, leading to the added tracks where the rail yard widened behind him. Stone wondered if Train Cop had organized any kind of search, and decided it would be better to be safe than sorry. The farther away from the rail yard he crossed the tracks, the better.

Lorne Street curved. On his right was a pleasant-looking park along the riverbank. Maybe he'd find a place there to sleep that night. Ahead, Lorne Street dipped to cross under the tracks.

Stone wanted to sprint, but knew it would draw unnecessary attention. So he ambled beneath the overpass, hands in his pockets. If Train Cop was watching or had other cops looking for him, they'd be looking for a kid with a red jacket, not tan. Not much protection, but he'd learned people weren't that observant, so probably enough.

He saw nothing to alarm him and headed to the comforting safety of the commercial area. Not soon enough. He was hungry. Very, very hungry. Not often did he have to puke twice between meals.

Chapter Nine

Stone had a credit card. Well, not a credit card. A credit-card number. It was legit. Well, legit but not in his name. His mother's name. Banks weren't keen on giving credit cards to fifteen-year-olds with no visible means of support. *Dealing ADHD meds* didn't look good as a job description on an application.

So he'd applied in his mom's name, lying about her income. When the card arrived he'd memorized the numbers, before cutting the card into pieces. That was almost as good as having the card itself. It didn't have much of a limit because his mom's credit score was crap, and he couldn't use the card anywhere except for Internet purchases because a woman's name was on it and merchants who looked would call in fraud if he tried using it in person. She didn't know about it. Otherwise, it would have been maxed out.

Having it also meant he could use a pay phone, punching in the credit-card number to make a long-distance call. It took him twenty minutes to find one.

A couple of beeps told him he'd navigated the instructions with success, and he heard the ringing. How did people live before cell phones anyway?

Didn't take long for an answer.

"Please put me on your do-not-call list," a girl said very precisely.

"It's Stone," he said.

"Stone? I don't recognize the area code. But you're lucky—I do recognize the voice. But wish you were a tele-marketer instead."

Her name was Violet. She loved hearing from telemarketers, hoping that after she asked them to put her on the do-not-call list, they'd make the mistake of calling her. That was her dream. Making millions by suing a telemarketer. She had rich parents, but that didn't matter. She wanted her own millions. Who didn't?

"Remember how I helped you get better grades during the school year?" Stone said.

"Help? I don't see it that way. I pay you twenty-five dollars per essay. You're not helping me. You're an employee."

"Remember you paid me to make sure your essays got a minimum B and nobody knew about it?"

"So this is blackmail?" Violet said. "You're the one who committed the crime. And those pills you sell—"

"Hey," Stone said. "Can I start over? I'm calling you because I need help."

"Really," Violet said, almost purring.

Yeah. A cat seeing a mouse trapped in a corner.

"I might be gone for a few days," Stone said. No way was he going to ask if she'd heard about anybody in East Hastings being hit by a van. She'd know the only reason he'd asked was because he must be involved, and the rest of the conversation would not go well.

"It's my mom," Stone said. "Somebody needs to check in on her, make sure she gets clean needles from the clinic down the street. I won't be able to do it for a while."

"I'm not that open to helping you," Violet said. "But I'd happily become an employee."

Stone sighed. Either way, this was going to cost him. He'd have to pay for help now or reduce his rates when he wrote essays for her during the upcoming school year. "Fair enough."

"Twenty-five bucks a visit," she said.

"What?" Stone heard his voice come out as a squeak.

"Who else you going to call?" she said. "Twenty-five bucks for each visit."

"Can I pay you by the week?" Stone was good with math. He knew to a penny what his savings account had. Hated spending. Someday he was going to own a Subway franchise. That was his ticket to a respectable life. "Seven days, seven visits. Seventy-five bucks guaranteed for the full week. You're giving me a discount rate for bulk."

She didn't answer. That made him a desperate negotiator.

"And if I'm back before the week is out," he continued, "you keep all seventy-five bucks, even if you don't visit seven times."

"Cash up front," Violet said.

"You do understand the concept of a different area code, right? Means I'm calling from outside your area code. Means I'm not close enough to get you the cash. Otherwise I'd visit her myself."

"Huh," she said. "Also means you really need me. Seventy-five bucks up front or you pay the full rate for a week. That would be…"

As she paused, he could picture the way her mouth opened and the way she pushed the tip of her tongue against her front teeth in concentration.

"That would be $105," he said. "And fine, I'll pay you that full rate."

"Deal," said Violet. "Hundred and five bucks cash when you see me."

He hung up. Her math was so bad he'd saved himself seventy dollars and was getting a bulk rate anyway.

He thought of school in the fall and the likelihood that Violet would come back to him for another essay. Rich kid with parents who demanded great grades. He'd bump his rate and make the money back by Christmas.

Chapter Ten

At McDonald's, Stone was glad to see how busy it was. That would make it easier to get food. But first he needed to clean up and take care of other important bodily functions. Getting rid of number one was easy enough outdoors, but not so much for another matter that had become pressing since escaping the rail yard.

On his way to the bathroom he scooped a copy of the *Vancouver Sun* from a pile on a side counter. For Stone, newspapers at McDonald's served two purposes. News and privacy.

In the bathroom, pressing matter finished and flushed, Stone folded the newspaper and made it into a wedge that he pushed under the door. That would keep anyone from walking in on him.

He then took off his jacket and shirt and did a quick sponge bath in the sink. He liked that this McDonald's had paper towel for hand drying instead of blowers. Paper towels made it so much more convenient to dry all the parts that needed drying.

Stone put his shirt back on and tucked it in. He slicked back his hair with water and checked himself out in the mirror. He practiced his earnest look and smiled with satisfaction. Time to get breakfast.

He pulled the newspaper wedge out from under the door and headed back to the main area with his jacket in one hand and the newspaper in the other.

He found a booth with a tray left behind by someone too lazy to bring it to the front. He set down his jacket and newspaper beside the tray. Then he walked to the opposite side of the restaurant. He leaned against the far wall and surveyed the tables. It took about thirty seconds to spot what he needed.

A family of four—a mom with three kids all under the age of seven. The kids were making the usual kid noises and squabbling the usual way that kids squabbled. The mom looked overwhelmed.

Stone walked back to his own table and picked up the dirty tray. He left his newspaper and jacket on the table.

With the dirty tray in hand, he walked up behind the woman and her three children as if he'd been sitting behind them.

He stopped at their table. She had a soccer-mom haircut and was patiently asking her children to use their napkins to wipe their faces.

"Hello," he said to the woman in his earnest voice. No British accent now. He pointed at the three trays on their table. "Things look crazy here. How about I help out? I'm headed to the garbage anyway."

"Thanks," she said, giving Stone a tired smile.

Stone leaned over the table. He picked up the empty wrappers and cups from all three trays and added them to his tray. Then he quickly moved all the leftover food onto one of the trays and slid the other two empty ones underneath his. Everything was now neatly sorted. Garbage on one tray. Leftovers on the other. "Have a nice day," he said brightly, and turned to go to the front of the restaurant with all the trays.

It was an abrupt turn, and he almost collided with someone who had been waiting behind him with his own tray.

The dude he had almost hit was big. Stone's face barely reached the dude's chest. A dude wearing a black hoodie and black pants. A dude with a black backpack.

Train Dude.

Stone didn't lift his head. He walked around.

Train Dude didn't try to stop him. Stone puzzled on that for a moment and then realized it made sense. Stone's face would have been in shadows in the boxcar, and Train

Dude probably didn't know what he looked like.

Stone continued to the front, where there was a place to stack trays and discard the garbage. He glanced back and saw the two things he needed to see.

Train Dude had taken a far booth and had his back to the restaurant, black hoodie still up. Stone had guessed right. He was safe.

Second thing was that Soccer Mom was too busy with her kids to be watching what Stone did with the trays. He dumped the garbage and put those trays in a stack, but kept the tray with the leftover food and made his way back to his own booth.

He pushed the food around to take a good look. Half of an egg biscuit. Nearly an entire pancake. And some hash browns. He checked to make sure that none of it had mustard on it.

It would be a good breakfast.

He opened the newspaper and began to search for any stories about a guy dying after being hit by a van in the East Hastings area.

Three pages into his search, Train Dude slid onto the bench on the other side of the booth. He plunked the black backpack down beside him.

Before Stone could scramble out of the booth, Train Dude clamped a hand firmly on Stone's wrist.

Stone looked up and finally saw inside Train Dude's hoodie.

Half the face was normal. The other half looked like the bubbled cheese on a pizza cooked a little too long.

Chapter Eleven

"I have a few questions for you," Train Dude said, his face mostly hidden in the hood but not hidden enough. His face was seriously messed up. "Lift your legs so that I can grab your feet."

"What's that, mate?" Stone said.

"You can knock off the phony British accent. I heard you talk normal to the woman and her kids. I said, give me your feet. Where I can grab them."

"What kind of weirdo are—"

"All I need to do is raise my voice and ask someone to call the cops," Train Dude said. "Or you can lift your feet and we have a conversation."

Stone lifted his feet. His shoes bumped against Train Dude's knees.

Train Dude used his other hand to clamp one of Stone's ankles. With a secure hold on Stone's ankle, Train Dude slid his first hand off Stone's wrist and clamped Stone's other ankle.

Stone had time to register horrible scarring across the top of Train Dude's hand too, scarring that matched his face. While he was thinking about this, he realized that Train Dude had untied his shoelaces. And now he was knotting the laces from both shoes together.

Train Dude dropped both of Stone's feet.

Not a bad move, Stone thought. Now there was no risk he'd run unless he left his shoes behind.

As soon as his feet hit the floor, Stone immediately popped his heels out of his shoes. But he wasn't going to run just yet. Train Dude hadn't called the cops, and Stone was curious enough about that to stay. Besides, he liked his shoes. Shoplifting wasn't easy, and getting the right size was always tough.

Train Dude stared at Stone.

Stone stared back, studying Train Dude's face. Now that he looked closer, Stone could see that the skin on the left side of the dude's face was swirly and waxy and marbled. Hideously tight across the one cheekbone. Stone thought it was no wonder Train Dude lived on trains, away from people.

Sigmund Brouwer

"That's a killer face for Halloween," Stone said. "Any other time, not so much."

"Most people look away," Train Dude said. "Sometimes little kids scream."

Stone was free of both of his shoes. He could escape any time.

"Fire?" Stone said. "Acid?"

"Fire," Train Dude said. "Looked worse before the surgeries."

Surgeries. As in plural.

Train Dude stared at Stone.

Stone stared back. He had a sudden surge of compassion for Train Dude, who didn't seem to pity himself. Tough to go through life looking at that in a mirror. Stone wouldn't extend pity though. Pity was different than compassion. Pity was a way of keeping power over a lesser person. Long time ago, he'd learned not to feel pity for himself. Hated it when people showed pity for him.

"I heard for operations like that sometimes they take skin from a person's butt," Stone said.

"They do," Train Dude said. "And did."

"People ever crack jokes about that?"

"You don't know me," Train Dude said, "and you ask something like that?"

"Thought the crack part was funny. You know, skin from a butt. Crack a joke. Crack?"

Train Dude just stared.

"We're going to pretend your face isn't messed up?" Stone asked.

Train Dude blinked and said, "I suppose, then, instead of laughing I could just crack a smile."

Stone snorted. "Good one." He let his chuckle fade. "Now that we're friends, maybe you'll let me go."

"I don't think so. Your turn to answer questions. Let's start with the fake accent."

At that moment Stone realized something. Back in the boxcar, Train Cop had called Stone *duke* before Stone had said a word.

"You sent the train cop to look for me. Told him I had a British accent."

"Walkie-talkie," Train Dude said in that rumbly low voice. "I know the office channel. Also told him to check with VPD for a misper. Vancouver Police Department. And misper. That's—"

"Yeah yeah," Stone said. No British accent. "Missing person. Next you'll explain to me what a B and E is. Like you haven't already figured out some things about me. What do you want to know? I'd like to go now."

Stone was playing in his mind how he'd make his escape. With his feet, he nudged his loose shoes on the floor toward the outer edge of the booth. He'd distract Train Dude somehow. Not with another mustard pill. Yes, public vomiting would create chaos. But little kids were at tables nearby. It would mess them up. Stone hated the sound of little kids crying, hated the thought of hurting little kids in any way.

Maybe he'd throw the tray in Train Dude's face, then stand and yell something like, *Pervert!* Grab his shoes and run out in sock feet, put the shoes on later when he had some safe distance between them.

"Let's start with a simple question," Train Dude said. "How far you think you'll get without your shoes?"

Before Stone could react, Train Dude slipped from his side of the booth and onto Stone's side.

Stone was trapped.

"Don't yell anything stupid," Train Dude said. "I just want a conversation."

"We could have had that last night," Stone said. "We had about a thousand miles together on the train."

"Two hundred thirty."

"Huh?" Stone said.

"Two hundred thirty miles. Three hundred sixty-eight kilometers. And I didn't feel like talking. Was having a peaceful evening until you showed up."

"Maybe I don't feel like talking now," Stone said.

"Train hopping is a federal crime," Train Dude said. "All I need to do is raise my voice and get a manager over here and ask him to make a phone call. Cops show up, and you're officially in the hands of social services. They can sort out what needs to be done. Sooner or later you'll talk. Might as well be to me. So tell me, why the train and where do you want to go?"

Chapter Twelve

Stone turned his body sideways and pushed up against the wall to make space between him and Train Dude. He stared hard, held Train Dude's eyes for a couple of beats, then looked away and spoke.

"Apparently, my old man had trouble finding the right kind of cigarette," he said, keeping his focus on the opposite side of the booth, as if the words were difficult to say. Acting had always been easy for Stone. It got him much of what he wanted in life. "He went out for a pack when I was two years old and never came back. My old lady finds a replacement for him more often than I change my socks. I thought this summer maybe I'd go look for my old man, deliver the smokes he went to the store to find and then kick him square in the—"

"I get the picture."

To Stone, it sounded like a good-enough lie. Just enough lack of self-pity and cynicism. There was a lot riding on whether he could sell this though. The danger of getting caught in a web of authorities was too high. The web would take him back to East Hastings, where a lot of bad things waited for him. He needed to stay away for a while. He'd make sure Violet checked in on his mother. All Stone would need to do was call his mom once a week to let her know he was still alive. Not that she noticed much when he didn't come home at night.

Stone felt good about his chances of convincing Train Dude why he'd jumped a train to cross the country. Stone had sold bigger lies before. Plenty of times.

What you needed was a kernel of truth in the lie. His dad really had said he was going to the store for cigarettes and had never returned. Probably stole the line from a bad country song. As for his mom, well, life in East Hastings was life in East Hastings. No father in the picture, less-than perfect mother. Those two parts of Stone's life were absolutely true. Besides, now that he thought about it, kicking his old man in the nuts had some appeal. If he couldn't go back to East Hastings, maybe he *should* go looking for his old man.

"Train is not a smart way to travel the country," Train Dude said. "It's illegal.

And it's dangerous. Even for people who know how to hop trains. It's clear to me that you don't. That's why I sent the cop after you. To protect you."

"Only way I could afford to do it," Stone said, looking back at Train Dude. "Can't pay for a bus ticket. Hitchhiking seemed more risky. I might run into the kind of weirdo who likes grabbing some kid's feet under a table at McDonald's and then trapping the kid in a booth. Heard of something called personal space?"

Train Dude sighed. "Really. You're not that funny."

"Yes," Stone said. "I am."

"How you'd get away from the CN cop?" Train Dude said. "I sent him right back to the boxcar."

"Here's what's really funny. I puked. Gave me enough time to get a head start. That's all I ever need. A head start."

"Puked. He scared you that bad?"

"It happens," Stone said. "Don't judge me."

"You in your teens yet?" Train Dude asked.

"Fifteen," Stone said.

"Sure," Train Dude said.

Ironic, Stone thought. People bought into his lies, but when he told the truth...

"So if I don't call the cops, then what?" Train Dude said.

"You go your way, I go mine."

"Kid your age needs someone responsible to help. I just watched you take leftover food from a table and pretend it was yours."

"Ever tried dumpster diving?" Stone said. "This way, I get it before it reaches the dumpster."

"How much money you have?"

"What I need."

Train Dude stared at Stone as if deep in thought.

Weird. Stone was already getting used to Train Dude's face. He stared back without flinching.

"You call the cops on me," Stone said, "first chance I get, I'll run away again. My school counselor says I have unresolved issues. I'm just trying to resolve it with Export 'A.'"

"Export 'A'?"

Obviously, Train Dude didn't smoke. If you wanted to sell a lie, you needed to give details. "Cigarettes. My old man's brand. Crazy, he keeps walking into stores that are fresh out. Otherwise I'm sure he would have been home a long time ago. I get him some Export 'A,' maybe he comes home."

Train Dude blinked, as if coming to a decision. "I need your name. And proof it's your name. Or cops and social services is your next stop."

It would be a bad thing for Stone to get involved with anyone official like cops. Back in Vancouver, he'd crashed a van, destroyed a parked car, fled the scene of an accident as an underage driver, run over someone and maybe killed him.

So it was an easy choice. Give up his name now and buy time for the moment he could make an escape.

"My name is Maxwell Hayden Stone," Stone said. "Library card good enough?"

"Yup."

Stone dug the card from his pocket. Handed it to him.

"So, Maxwell—" Train Dude said, handing it back.

"Stone," Stone interrupted. "Since first grade, no one's called me anything but Stone. You happy now?"

"Not really." Train Dude sighed. "Where exactly does your old man live?"

"Last I heard was Winnipeg. But why should you care?"

"Because the only way I can think of to make sure you get back home safe is to first help you find him."

"That's a lot of bother," Stone said. "A waste of your time."

Train Dude said, "I ride the rails because all I've got is time with nothing else to do. And I'm heading east anyway."

Chapter Thirteen

Five minutes later they were outside the McDonald's. Stone knew he could outrun Train Dude. Stone could outrun anyone.

He eyed a narrow alley and was just about to bust his best move when Train Dude said, "First thing we have to do is buy you some gear."

"Gear?" Stone settled back on his heels.

"Suppose you could go ahead and make a run for that alley," Train Dude said. "I'm not going to chase you. I've made my offer to help, and if you don't take it, I call the cops and walk away guilt-free, knowing I did my best. Or you could come along with me and get the answer to your question."

"Question?"

"About gear," Train Dude said.

"Wasn't thinking of running."

Train Dude slowly shifted his face inside the hoodie to stare at Stone.

"Okay," Stone said. "I was."

"Only one way to find out what I meant about gear." Train Dude started to walk without looking back.

Stone felt like a stupid puppy as he followed the big man. "Hey," he said to Train Dude's back. "What's *your* name?"

"You going to run? Don't want to bother giving you a name if I'm just wasting my time."

Crap, Stone thought. Now Train Dude was extending some kind of trust. Like he was going to take Stone's word for it. Stone didn't want someone to trust him. Too much responsibility. That alone was a good-enough reason to bolt while he could.

But Stone realized now that maybe he did want to find his old man, and maybe he did want to unleash some serious anger on the guy for running out on him. And Train Dude was big and calm and had a strange kind of peace to him for someone who had been turned into a freak by fire. Stone didn't mind the feeling of safety around the guy. Stone also needed to kill a lot of time before it was safe to go back to Vancouver— as long as Violet was looking in on his mother while he was gone. Maybe Stone wouldn't run for good. Yet.

"You're not some kind of pervert?"

"If I was, I'd tell you I wasn't."

"Very helpful. Thanks."

"Think about it. Tell me how you know I'm not."

"Yeah yeah," Stone said. "You'd have tried something last night when you had me trapped in the boxcar. Had to ask. Hate for my elementary teachers to have put up all those *Stranger Danger* posters in the hallways for nothing."

"Was kind of hoping you wouldn't be a talker," Train Dude said, not turning his head.

"You knew better when you asked for proof of my identification," Stone said, talking to the man's back. "Saw me talk my way right into breakfast."

"Just glad you've dropped the phony British accent."

For Stone, the accent was a form of disguise. It came in handy, like a reversible coat. Plus it made him feel like more than a street rat from East Hastings.

"Wouldn't you like to know why I use different accents and how I learned them from YouTube?"

"Not interested," Train Dude said. "Really. Just follow me and concentrate on breathing. From here on in, you get one question a day."

Stone followed.

Sun felt hot. Must have been really hot for Train Dude, wearing all black. Six blocks, Stone followed. It was the part of town with businesses lining each side of the street. Hair salons. Drugstores. Chinese restaurants. Dry cleaners. Stone felt at home here. Lots of people, lots of pavement, lots of smells like car exhaust. Not once did

Train Dude turn to see if he was there. Stone felt like a small car following in the draft of a massive semitruck.

Stone wanted to ask where they were going. But he wasn't going to waste his remaining question of the day on that, because he'd get the answer soon enough. He followed the black shadow and concentrated on breathing.

Finally, the man turned into the parking lot of a used-sporting-goods store. "You still there?" he asked without looking back.

"Yeah."

"Follow me inside or wait out here," Train Dude said. "But I don't want chatter. I like to get in and out of stores as fast as I can. Fewer kids who scream at the sight of my face, the better."

"Got it," Stone said. "Inside. Air conditioning. No chatter."

"One other thing," Train Dude said. "It's Nelson."

"What?" Stone asked.

"You wanted my name. Nelson. Joseph Nelson. Never Joe. Since first grade, always Joseph."

Chapter Fourteen

Earlier, when Stone had left the train yard at a run, he'd gone left, keeping the tracks between him and the river. As it turned out, had he gone right, he would have ended up in Pioneer Park.

That was the spot—about a fifteen-minute walk from the used-sporting-goods store—where they stopped after the shopping spree.

After paying at the cash register with a debit card, Joseph had grunted and pointed at the bags. Stone had taken the hint. It was his job to carry the bags while he followed the black backpack and black hoodie until they reached the park.

Joseph stopped at a fountain and drank deeply, then found a bench in the shade of a tree. Stone drank from the fountain too, then joined Joseph.

In front of them was river, where the green of the park grass melted into the sand of a beach, and little kids were making themselves gritty under the watch of moms under umbrellas. To the left, the dull drone of traffic crossing the bridge over the river. To the right, the *thwack* of tennis balls against rackets from courts on the other side of the trees. Stone wondered what that would be like, to have a life where you could afford to knock a ball over a net simply to keep track of how many times you succeeded or failed.

"You need to sort out the gear," Joseph said.

"Probably hot in there," Stone said.

"In where?"

"That hood. Your face won't bother me. My mom's a drug addict. Takes a lot to mess with my head."

Joseph grunted. Stone couldn't tell what the grunt meant, but Joseph pulled back the hood and shook out his hair, long and black.

No denying, Stone thought, the dude's face was a wreck.

"Start with the backpack," Joseph said.

"The one I could have used when we left the store instead of carrying it in a bag?" Stone said. "Wouldn't have minded doing that a lot earlier. Like, in the parking lot of the store."

"We draw less attention by sorting through it here," Joseph said. "Except for the hiking boots and the new clothes that you'll wear, everything goes in it. It's your gear, so pack it the way you want. My advice, though, is put heavy stuff on the bottom. Easier to keep your balance when you're running for a train."

Stone knew what he'd find in the other shopping bags. In the store he'd watched Joseph throw stuff in the cart. Gloves, boots, blanket, rain sheet, cutlery, sunblock, toothbrush, black pants, black hoodie. And a walkie-talkie, which explained the squawking Stone had heard earlier from Joseph's backpack. Apparently, Stone was going to become a mini Joseph. Better-looking though.

"Can't pay you back for this," Stone said.

"That sucks. I was saving up for a house so I could live in one place and every day watch everyone in the neighborhood try to avoid looking at my face."

The sarcasm didn't sound bitter. Just matter-of-fact.

"Maybe any color but black would help you fit in," Stone said.

"Black is invisible at night," Joseph answered. "Bulls can't see you."

"Because we're ranchers." Stone didn't want to frame it like a question. He had no doubt that Joseph would stick to his word about one question a day.

"*Bull* is a train-yard cop."

"With an office channel you call when convenient."

"Need the walkie-talkie to listen in on crew changes and best time to jump a train." Joseph frowned. At least, it looked to Stone like a frown. "Where'd you get that?"

Stone had reached into his pocket and pulled out an expensive folding knife.

"Nice, huh?" Stone said, bouncing sunlight off the blade. "Should come in handy."

"That doesn't answer my question," Joseph said. "I asked you where you got it."

"Same place you got all this gear. I can go back and get you one. Paid a lot less than you did for stuff. Like, zero."

"You and me, we may be through then," Joseph said. "Even before we get started."

"You're kidding." Stone was startled at that. And startled to find himself disappointed. This had begun to feel like a real adventure.

"I don't steal," Joseph said.

"You have money," Stone answered. "I don't."

"Even more reason not to steal. Doing the right thing when it's easy doesn't prove anything."

"I'm not interested in doing the right thing. I'm interested in surviving."

"Then survive without me."

"You're kidding," Stone said again.

"Absolutely not."

"Gear is yours then," Stone said. One thing Stone never did was beg. "Hope you kept the receipt." He stood up from the bench.

"Hang on," Joseph said. He put a hand in his front pocket and came out with folded money. Looked like hundred-dollar bills. He peeled two of them off the stack and offered the bills to Stone. He also handed Stone the store receipt.

"Take it. You pack the gear, take it with you, go back to the store, pay for the knife, apologize to the manager, then you and me, we're good. We ride together, look for your old man."

"Knife didn't cost two hundred."

"That's in case you decide you'd rather be a thief. In case you decide not to do the right thing—pay for it and apologize. Then you're clear from my conscience with enough money to survive and gear you can keep or turn in for more money. You don't come back, it's a small price to pay to find out I can't trust you."

Stone took the money, thinking about candies and babies and the easiness of this.

"I need to be away from you right now," Joseph said. "I'm so mad I might say something I regret."

Joseph flipped his hood back over his head, lifted his backpack and headed for another bench.

That left Stone alone with all his gear, the receipt for it and the money. What he should do was throw the money down and walk away from it all.

He didn't need to take self-righteous crap from anyone.

Apologize and come back? Hardly.

Angry as he was, though, Stone wasn't going to let raw emotion force him into a stupid decision.

Best revenge, Stone decided, would be to take everything, the gear and the money.

If he hung on to the gear and went his own way—maybe wait a day or two and get on a train by himself—two hundred bucks could go a long way. Maybe Stone could still find his old man and kick him in the nuts.

Yeah. He could do all this without Freak Face around to judge him.

Chapter Fifteen

It took Stone until just after dark to come to a decision. It was this: If Freak Face said a single word in satisfaction or triumph at Stone's return, then Stone would turn around and walk. With the dude's two hundred dollars and all the gear in the backpack.

This decision was based on the fact that a half hour before dark—just before the store closed at 9:00 PM—Stone had walked inside, asked for the manager, paid for the folding knife and apologized for stealing it in the first place.

All day, it had been like a burr wedged between his butt cheeks, telling him it needed to be done. He'd gone to the library, found nothing about any hit-and-run deaths in Vancouver the night before. But that didn't ease his worry. Van Dude could be on life support and that wouldn't make the papers. Even so, there was the fact that he'd driven with no license, caused an accident and made it a hit-and-run. VPD would want him bad, even if Van Dudes didn't. And Van Dudes would, no matter what the newspapers did or didn't report.

He'd tried calling Violet from a pay phone to get an update about his mom— he'd had to go back to the original pay phone because he couldn't find another one—but got no answer. Three times he'd walked into Walmart to buy a pre-paid cell with the cash from Freak Face, and three times he'd walked out, not sure why he couldn't bring himself to spend any part of the two hundred.

At a playground late that afternoon, he'd spotted a woman with a baby in a stroller, chatting on her iPhone. She'd gasped at a toddler about to climb a swing set, dropped the phone and run to rescue the kid, leaving the stroller unprotected. It would have been easy enough to walk past, grab the woman's wallet from her open purse on top of the stroller and keep going. Maybe take the phone too, keep it unlocked and get what he could out of it until she reported it stolen. Babies made it so much easier to steal.

Yet he'd avoided the temptation. With self-disgust at his weakness of character, Stone had made a last-second decision to leave the wallet alone.

Instead of an easy theft, Stone had kicked the stroller instead, taking satisfaction that the baby in it had woken up and begun to wail.

After that he'd found himself walking past the sporting-goods store again and again, telling himself that no way was he going inside to pay for the knife, let alone apologize for stealing it in the first place.

So he'd hung out in the parking lot as the shadows got longer and longer. When he'd seen a guy in a dress shirt and tie walk up to lock the door, some idiot impulse drove him to run up and ask him if he was the manager.

What irritated Stone even more happened after the apology. The manager had passed along a message to Stone, saying some guy had called the store earlier to ask the manager to tell the kid who stole the knife to go back to the same bench at 10:00 PM and call channel 24 if there was any trouble along the way.

In other words, Stone showing up at the bench would prove he'd actually done what Freak Face considered the right thing to do. Now, in the cool evening air, walking to Pioneer Park to be at the bench on time, Stone was feeling mad at Freak Face for once again forcing Stone to live up to a responsibility of trust that Stone had not asked for and did not want.

So that was his decision. If Freak Face said anything about any of this when Stone got to the bench, Stone was gone. He hadn't apologized for stealing to please Freak Face. He didn't know why he'd bothered, and he didn't want to spend any time thinking about it, or be reminded about it by Freak Face.

It took him until he reached the park to realize that, angry as he was, at least that burr wedged between his butt cheeks was gone.

There was no one at the bench.

He sat.

A large black shape appeared, silent except for two words. "Let's go."

Chapter Sixteen

"It's hot and I'm sweating," Stone said. "Maybe I should just put this jacket into my backpack again."

"You'll get cold later, and taking it out of the backpack is not so easy when the train is moving," came the answer.

A half hour after leaving the park, Stone was in the same train yard he'd fled that morning. He now saw the wisdom of dark clothing. He followed Joseph, barely able to see the man even though he was only a couple of steps ahead.

The train cars were massive hulks beside them, and Stone felt that if he spoke too loud, they'd wake up and smother him into the gravel.

The world Stone had left behind was noise and chaos and moving lights. Here was too much darkness, too much silence. Spooky. Very spooky.

Then, like out of a horror film, two flashlight beams suddenly appeared.

Stone ducked underneath a flatbed car, expecting Joseph to do the same. Joseph moved toward him, but not to hide.

Instead, Joseph grabbed his arm and yanked him away from safety.

"Told you to do as I do," Joseph grunted.

"But—"

"Kid last year thought stopped cars never roll. He was wrong. Lost both legs below his knees. Never, I mean *never*, go beneath couplers or cars."

The flashlights were closer.

"Yard bulls," Stone said. "Didn't you say we needed to avoid them?"

"Said to do as I do. That should be enough, Max. Now try to make it through the next minute or two without talking."

"Name's not Max," Stone said under his breath. "It's Stone."

Plus he was hot. But mentioning it again would be complaining. Stone didn't like complainers, so he tried not to be one himself.

Joseph kept a firm grip on Stone's shoulder, then raised his voice.

"Couple travelers out in front of you," he called out. "Thought I'd give you plenty of warning."

The flashlight beams snapped toward Joseph's voice. The spillover light blinded Stone.

"Here for the crew change on that Calgary express," Joseph said in an even voice. "Hoping to catch a 53. Chances good?"

Both flashlight beams kept a steady approach.

Stone smelled a cigarette.

"It's him," one of the voices said, flashlight sweeping high across Joseph's face. "Legend. Right? That's you? Silent good deeds and moving on. Some of the new guys don't believe you're real. You're the legend."

The other guy knocked the beam down. "Moron. That's not something you ask."

"Any 53s?" Joseph asked. "Getting old. Looking for luxury. Calgary express on time?"

"Slight delay," the first voice said, almost in deference. "Some kind of hitch on paperwork. But yeah, you'll find some 53s."

Second voice said, "Been a while. Some of the new guys, like this idiot, don't believe you're real. All good these days?"

"All good." Joseph was digging in his coat pocket. He came out with a pack of cigarettes. There was enough light from the flashlights for Stone to notice it was Export 'A.' Huh.

"Spent a couple years in the south-west," Joseph said. "Nice weather. The train riders, though, are a different breed. Got tired of listening to them talk about American politics."

"Everybody is," the second voice chuckled.

Joseph tossed the pack toward the flashlight beams, now maybe a couple of steps away. Stone heard a slight smack. Not the smack of it hitting the ground, but of it hitting a palm.

"Thanks," a voice said.

Then the beams moved away.

"Um…" Stone began.

"Yard bulls are the ones you worry about," Joseph said. "Guys who work the yard, they're okay mostly. If the yard bull wasn't having a snooze in his office, I'd hear it on the radio. That answer your question?"

"Not sure you could call it a question because I didn't really get the words out," Stone said, thinking about what he'd heard. *Legend. Some of the new guys don't believe you're real.*

"That's all you get, Max. Let's find that 53 before the express starts to shake."

Chapter Seventeen

It turned out there was a good reason Joseph had insisted Stone wear clothing that seemed too hot. They were now five hours into the train ride—the last time Joseph had spoken was just after the train began to roll, and just three words—*don't fall off.*

The train was going maybe ninety kilometers an hour, and the high elevation and wind sucked away the warmth. Stone wasn't shivering, but he also wasn't far from shivering. He couldn't imagine how close to freezing he'd have been with just the clothes he'd been wearing when he left East Hastings.

And it turned out that a 53 meant a flatbed with C-Can 52s, large shipping containers fifty-two feet long. It also turned out that the flatbed had an extra foot of margin to make it easier to drop the C-Can in place, which is why it was called a 53.

That was about all Stone had been able to get from Joseph before the train started to move. They had settled in on the back side of the C-Can, resting their backs against the steel wall, legs hanging over the couplings below.

This was luxury?

Not to Stone. The train was shaking and screaming on the rails. Loud topped out at full speed somewhere in the dark in the mountains.

It was very dark. The train was wreathed in fog. Or maybe cloud, it had climbed so high.

"Not going to be like this," Stone shouted to Joseph. "Us going places, you thinking I'm a piece of baggage with legs. Hear me? I'm not a minion."

Would have been much easier, Stone thought, if Joseph had had the decency to explain ahead of time the difference between yard workers and a yard bull, or that having a walkie-talkie tuned in to the yard frequency was all they needed to protect themselves from the CN cops.

But no, Joseph had walked them past a bunch of different-looking freight cars, from tankers to something he grunted was just a grainer, ignoring all of Stone's questions.

"I'm not your punk," Stone shouted. "Got that?"

Still no answer. Not above the shaking and rattling and the sound of steel wheels against steel rails.

With no warning the whistling, screaming sounds changed into an echoing blast, and the gray fog disappeared and the air turned to soot.

What the —!

Stone realized the train had entered a tunnel. Like, thanks for the warning, Freak Face, he thought.

He held his breath.

The tunnel didn't end.

He coughed. He dragged soot into his lungs with his next gasp for air. He held his breath again. And again. And again.

The tunnel still didn't end.

Not for twenty minutes.

When cold air hit him again and he saw starlight, it was almost as if the tunnel world had been real and this new world wasn't.

But wow, what an amazing unreal world. On this side of the mountain, the air was clear. The sky so black that starlight seemed to stab Stone's eyes.

And moonlight.

Enough to show him the ridges of the jagged mountaintops.

Stone had never seen a world like this, never known something so big and hauntingly beautiful—even with the constant scream of steel against steel—could exist. Like East Hastings was just a dirty bubble.

Still, East Hastings was *his* bubble. Sooner or later, he'd need to get answers to more than one question a day. Thinking about this added to Stone's irritation.

So he shouted at Joseph again. "And another thing. Stop calling me Max!"

No surprise, Freak Face didn't answer.

Chapter Eighteen

"Lake Louise!" It came as a shout from Joseph.

"I didn't ask!" Stone shouted back. Even though he'd been wondering and would have asked if he thought Joseph could hear him. "Not if I only get one question a day. Not wasting it on something like that."

"Lake water's that color because of dissolved minerals."

Either the guy couldn't hear or he was ignoring the point Stone was trying to make.

"Really?" Stone shouted. "Your first words in ten hours and that's what you give me? A tour-guide spiel? And that wasn't my question because I don't expect an answer."

But his words didn't come out with much anger or attitude, especially compared to how Stone had felt the night before. Hard to stay mad when you were afraid to blink in case the unreal world disappeared.

He had thought the mountain ridges and starlight were awesome. But this. Wow. In early sunlight, this kind of magic sucked the air from a person's lungs.

The lake was jewel. A. Jewel.

The moving train was even with it, giving Stone the panoramic view.

Aquamarine water. A mirror surface, tucked in a bowl of mountains. Brilliant white snow topping those mountains, brilliant blue sky framing those mountains.

Postcard. Yeah. He'd seen this on postcards. But now he knew that was like the difference between smelling a steak and taking a bite.

Snarkiness seemed so, so tiny in the face of all this. His heart wasn't into delivering any kind of attitude.

Hadn't hurt that Joseph had just placed his backpack between his knees, held it steady against the shaking of the train and pulled out a couple of sandwiches, offered one to Stone.

Stone had been awake most of the night, staring at the sky, blown away by how big the world was. All that fresh air made a person hungry.

"Hey," Stone shouted. "Tastes great. Thanks."

Joseph turned that melted face to Stone and smiled. The smile surprised Stone, how good it looked.

"You're welcome, Max."

Yeah, Stone thought, the guy had heard every word he'd said so far on the back of this 53. Every word.

And stop calling me Max, Stone thought too. But he didn't say it. The lake looked too good. The sandwich tasted too great. He'd save that fight for later.

All in all, Stone felt better than he'd felt in days. He gave that some thought. Actually, he felt better than he had in months.

That good feeling lasted until the amputation in the train yard in Calgary, another three hours down the line.

Chapter Nineteen

"Good things in life take time," Joseph said. This was after the amputation, when they were leaving Calgary on an eastbound grain hopper. "It's the bad things that happen quickly, like car accidents and train crashes."

Stone, looking at the scars on Joseph's face, wondered how often the man had those kind of thoughts. A bad face like that happened in a flash. Literally.

Stone kept his thoughts to himself and just listened. He was getting better at that.

"Just about every good in life," Joseph continued, "like building character or reputation or strength or relationships, takes time. Sure, bad things can happen just as slowly as good things," he acknowledged. "Bad things like cancer. But bad is about the only thing you should expect to happen in an instant."

Stone wanted to argue just for the sake of arguing. Except he was remembering the amputation, and that's how he was going to remember it for a long time. Something that happened so quickly, you really didn't realize what had happened until there was a foot dangling by skin from the rest of the leg. Difficult to unsee.

It had happened when they were out of the mountains surrounding Lake Louise, out of the foothills, and onto the first hint of the prairies. The inbound train was moving maybe two or three kilometers an hour into the train yard of downtown Calgary.

Trains took a long time to come to a stop. Stone still couldn't really get his head around how much a loaded freight train weighed, how much force it took to get it moving and to stop it again. At three kilometers an hour, he thought, it would still smash through a concrete building like it was a house of cards.

At the same time, an outbound was headed west back to the mountains, picking up speed.

Stone had been looking upward at the Calgary Tower, so thin from the base to the top and then with what looked like an upside-down teacup for a crown.

As he glanced down, a small movement caught his eye.

Some dude, running alongside the outbound, reaching for a handrail. No different than when Stone had been desperate to do so back in Vancouver.

Just as his brain was assembling that image came the next. The dude slipping, mouth opening wide with a scream that was lost in the rumble of freight cars. Looked like his leg had gone under.

Stone had been trying to decide if the image had been real when he'd caught more movement.

Joseph, dropping down with his backpack, landing hard on gravel, but spinning to dash toward the fallen dude.

Stone did the same. Slow as the train was moving, he still stumbled. Deceptive, the forces at work. His own backpack bumped him hard. He took a breath and ran toward Joseph.

Stone reached the two of them. The westbound was still moving. How could it have stopped? Who knew the train needed stopping? And if someone knew, the same massive weight that rolled above those steel wheels would have needed a kilometer, maybe two, to finally come to rest. By then the dude would have bled out.

Stone looked down at the dude's leg, then away. The foot was still there, but at a crazy angle. Blood shot in weird spurts and formed small pools.

"Coat," Joseph said. Joseph didn't yell. There was a surreal calm to Joseph's voice, but it carried authority. "Max. Your coat. Now."

Stone fumbled with the zipper of his backpack. He came out with the coat. He didn't understand why Joseph needed the coat until he watched the big man rip shreds of cloth away from it.

Stone's pill bottle tumbled out of the coat pocket. Joseph ignored it. He used a strip of cloth to tie the dude's leg just below the knee. The spurts lessened.

Another strip. Another loop tied, this time lower on the dude's leg. Four strips in total by the time Joseph finished.

Stone was mesmerized by something else though. The dude was unconscious now, clearly in shock, gasping instead of screaming.

"Stay with him," Joseph said.

"Me," Stone said. This was too much responsibility.

Barely a few feet away, the train kept moving past them. Stone didn't have to strain to hear Joseph. That calm authority cut through all the noise.

"Yeah, you," Joseph said. "I'm going down the tracks to radio this in. If he wakes, he's going to need to know help is on the way. He's going to need to know that the bleeding has stopped, and he's going to make it."

"Radio it from here," Stone said. "What if he starts bleeding again?"

"After what just happened to him, you want him to wake up to a face like mine and think he died and went to hell?"

Joseph didn't give Stone a chance to reply. He turned and headed down the tracks.

Stone scooped the pills back into his pocket and waited for help.

Chapter Twenty

Some ten hours later, somewhere past Medicine Hat and headed to Regina, Stone and Joseph were on a stretch where the train had slowed to barely more than a walking pace. As far as Stone could see, there wasn't a single tree. Barely even any shrubs. Just limitless land with gentle swells, with grass more brown than green.

"Is this what the rest of Canada is like?" Stone asked. Then he immediately said, "Cancel that. It wasn't my question for today."

"That one's easy enough to answer. It won't count as your question. Prairie from here to just past Winnipeg. In places, like this, it's unbroken grassland. Then some places it's as flat as a table, with wheat and other planted grains. Just past Winnipeg, in what seems like a snap of the fingers, you hit trees and rocks and lakes. Called the Canadian Shield. Thousand kilometers of it. Other side, farmlands of Ontario, except for the bloat that's Toronto and the area around it. Then the St. Lawrence. Big ships. After that, trees again. Until you hit ocean. Ocean. Too bad for you that you won't be going past Winnipeg."

"Yeah," Stone said. "Too bad."

Maybe he didn't really want to find his father and kick him in the nuts. Maybe he'd just keep riding rail. In East Hastings, he hadn't known any other world could exist. Out here, East Hastings no longer seemed real.

"Let's talk about the pills you've been hiding," Joseph said. Back in Calgary, Stone had thought Joseph hadn't noticed. Wrong.

Joseph continued, "I didn't see any scrip on the bottle."

Scrip. Short for *prescription*. The guy wasn't a stranger to the streets. Or to the implications of a plain pill container.

"You addicted?" Joseph asked. "Or do you deal? Or both."

His tone suggested that Stone had better not be dealing. Or addicted. Or both.

Stone said, "My mom and me. We moved into our last apartment, the place smelled of mold and cat pee. First thing I did was scrub it down with Lysol. Second thing I did was buy a couple gallons of paint. Didn't really have a choice in color. Had to buy paint that somebody had tinted and then changed their minds. Turned out to be a snot green. Could see why they'd changed their minds. That was okay with me though. Spent thirty bucks on paint instead of a hundred fifty. Anything was better than the way the apartment looked when we moved in."

Stone didn't mention that he'd stolen the paint rollers. Clearly, Joseph was sensitive to that kind of thing.

"So now we live in an apartment that's snot green," Stone said, "but it doesn't smell of cat pee and mold. When I'm doing homework at night, I wear earbuds and listen to Beethoven. Hard to believe, I bet. Beethoven. I heard it helps you concentrate better. Any idea what my grades are?"

There was enough of a breeze to make it comfortable on the train. Joseph shrugged.

"Nothing lower than 100 percent. I mean it. Nothing lower," Stone said. "Some subjects, it's more than 100 percent because of bonus marks. The other reason I wear earbuds with Beethoven cranked is I don't want to hear my mom crying. Drugs have messed her up pretty bad. So no, I'm not addicted. I've seen what it does to someone. Those are scrip."

"No label that I saw."

"I do have a prescription," Stone said. "It's for ADHD. It's not in a drug-store container because where I come from, stealing the scrip information is almost as good as getting the pills."

"ADHD."

"I didn't say I have it. I said it's for it. Never take them myself."

"Ran a con job on a psychologist?" Joseph asked.

Crap, Stone thought. This guy was good.

"Maybe," Stone said. Con job had been easy to run. All it took was a little Internet research. Stone made good money on those pills. Rich kids loved how it calmed them and helped them concentrate. Stone didn't need help concentrating. Every day was a tightrope act. You never got bored or lazy walking a tightrope.

"So being poor is a reason to lie and steal and sell drugs?"

"Being hungry to bust away from that life is a reason. Someday I'm going to run my own business, own a house. I hate waking up to cockroaches crawling across the floor. Hate it."

Joseph said nothing after that. Maybe a half hour of prairie passed by the two of them, legs dangling off the end, train moving slow. Stone never knew a sky could be so big.

"I've got today's question," Stone said. He wanted to ask Joseph about the fire and the bad thing that had happened in a flash, but sensed the only way he'd hear about it was if Joseph volunteered it. He also wanted to ask Joseph about life on the trains, how long he'd been doing it. And if Stone was one of Joseph's good deeds.

It's him, one of the voices behind the flashlight had said. *Legend. Right? That's you. Silent good deeds and moving on*.

Stone wanted to ask all those things. Instead, what came out was, "You said you'd be able to find my father's address. How?"

"Wrong question," Joseph said. "So I'll give you the answer you really want instead."

He dug into his backpack and found his phone. He squinted to read the screen.

"You were right that he lived in Winnipeg," Joseph said. "Instead of asking how I'd be able to find his address, you should have asked what it was. So here's the answer—1012 Beaver Lodge Street. Northeast corner of the city. We can stay on this train, and we'll hit the train yard in Winnipeg tomorrow morning before the sun rises. From there, you'll be on your own."

Chapter Twenty-One

By the rising numbers on a street of duplexes as he walked, Stone easily guessed that 1012 Beaver Lodge was on the far corner.

The late-morning sun showed that one half of the duplex had fresh white paint on wood siding, a neat lawn. The other side looked twice the age, with cracked yellow paint and patchy grass.

The nice half had curtains. The bad half had tinfoil to block the sunlight.

The nice half was not 1012.

Yeah, Stone thought, no fairy-tale reunion here. It was at that moment that Stone realized he hadn't come this far because he wanted to kick the old man in the groin. He'd been hoping to find a house with fresh paint and a neat lawn and curtains. In a house like that, there would be a man who regretted leaving a son behind, a man who would embrace the long-lost son, shed a manly tear of regret and try to find a way to make up for lost years.

He paused on the sidewalk, wondering if it would even be worth it to knock on the door.

He knew the answer. Stone wasn't going to walk away without at least seeing the dude who'd walked away from him for a pack of Export 'A.'

As he steeled himself to go up the walk, the decision was taken away from him.

The door banged opened, and a scrawny terrier-type dog bolted outside.

An equally scrawny man stopped in the doorway and called back into the house, loud enough for his words to reach Stone. He was carrying a can of beer. "Think I give a crap? Stick your head in the oven for all I care."

The man wore brown pants and a black AC/DC T-shirt spotted with various stains. He hacked a cough and spit brownish gob onto the top of the steps.

Beautiful, Stone thought.

By then the terrier had made it to the center of the lawn and was already straining in the peculiar posture of a dog forcing out a load. There were plenty of other loads in various stages of decay around it.

"What you staring at?" the man asked Stone. "Never seen a dog take a dump before?"

"Friend in Vancouver sent me," Stone said. "Wanted me to give you some money. To come visit him and his mom."

"Sure," the man said, hacking out more spit. "Vancouver. Like I know anyone in Vancouver with money. Let me guess. I'm going to need to sign for it. Nice try. That only worked once. Nobody's been able to slap me with proof of a delivered court order since."

"Friend's name is Maxwell Stone. Mother's name is Marlene. You know her?"

The terrier had finished. Stone was impressed at the size of the pile from such a little dog. The terrier sniffed the lawn in a few different spots, then made a straight line for the door. As it passed by the man, he tried to kick it, but the dog was expecting it and easily dodged the blow. That's when Stone realized the man was half drunk.

"Yeah," the man said. "I know her. Big dreams of being an actress. Made me take her out to Vancouver and promised that when she made it big, I'd be along for the ride. She didn't. So here I am."

He took a swig from the beer can. A startled look crossed his face as he tilted it completely, probably surprised that it was empty.

"She still go by the last name Stone?" The guy burped and tossed the empty can onto the grass. "If so, that's the only thing of mine I left behind for her."

Chapter Twenty-Two

"And money?" the man continued, weaving a bit. "Why you lying to me? She's got no money. Last time I checked, she was on the streets. Big actress dream didn't turn out that good. Otherwise I would have gone back for my share of the money. Anyone could see it wasn't going to happen. No sense in hanging around. So this money, if it's real, didn't come from her."

Stone supposed he could have asked for identification to prove the man in front of him was his father, that Joseph had given him the right address. But what were the odds this guy would have two facts right? That she was on the streets and had wanted to be an actress.

"The money belongs to my friend. He's got stuff happening on the street. Too much stuff to travel out here himself. So he sent me. Wants to see you." Stone took a breath. "My friend said you were his father."

"Give me the money," the man said. "Sure, I'll visit. Better be enough cash for me to fly. Plus some extra for the time it takes to look the kid in the face and tell him not to bother coming to me for anything. When I walked, I walked."

"He said before I gave you the money to make sure you proved you were the guy he wanted to see. Said you should tell me what color you painted the rocking horse you gave him for Christmas once."

"Never gave the kid a rocking horse. Never gave the kid a damn thing. Must have been Marlene lying to him, making up stories. Never saw the kid grow out of diapers. But hand over the money. I'll visit, show my face, let him decide for himself. Flight's going to cost minimum six hundred bucks, I'd say. Another four hundred for my time. The kid rich? Running dope?"

Stone had never intended to kick the man. What he had really planned was to vomit on the guy if he didn't seem concerned about running out on Stone. This guy clearly had no remorse. Stone reached into his pocket for a mustard pill. He slipped it into his mouth.

Puking on the guy would be better than kicking him in the groin.

"You got kids here?" Stone asked. If so, he felt plenty sorry for those kids.

"No way. Learned my lesson the first time," the man said. "They're a pain. Worse than a yappy dog."

Stone moved a little closer. Smelled the stink of the man and his unwashed T-shirt. Heard the television blaring inside the house.

That's when Stone realized something. The kind of man who would run out on a child was not the kind of man you'd want around to raise you in the first place. Sure, it would have been nice to have a normal dad and a normal childhood. But Stone hadn't been in on that kind of luck, so the next best thing was to have grown up without the jerk standing in front of him. In a way, that was lucky too. Some kids had no choice but to be stuck with a dad who messed them up big-time. At least Stone didn't have to live with the guy in his life.

"Hey," Stone said. He lifted his hand and discreetly spit the mustard pill into his palm, and as he dropped his hand, he let it fall onto the ground. "Got to go. But it was great to meet you."

It really was. A huge burden had lifted off Stone. He would never again wonder about his missing father.

"What about the money?"

"I'm going to tell my friend you weren't worth meeting."

Stone walked.

Then stopped.

He'd forgotten something.

He reached into his pocket. Found the pack of Export 'A.'

He turned around.

The man was scowling at him.

"I was supposed to deliver these too," Stone said, holding them out.

"Better than nothing, I suppose." The guy showed his jagged yellow teeth, probably thinking the rest of the world would believe it was a smile. He reached for the package in Stone's hand.

Stone tossed the cigarettes onto the lawn. It hadn't been intentional, but it felt good seeing it land in that fresh pile of dog poop.

A dozen steps or so later, Stone turned around. The guy was carefully lifting the cigarettes out of the poop.

Yup, Stone thought, definitely a good thing to not have someone like that in his life.

Chapter Twenty-Three

Best choice was boxcars, Stone reminded himself, hearing Joseph's calm voice in his mind.

He'd been walking steadily to the Winnipeg train yard, passing streets with names like St. James and Ellice and Portage.

It was hot. Hard to believe stories about how cold Winnipeg was in the winter.

As he walked, Stone ran a mental list, in the order that Joseph had taught him. If not boxcar, the rear platform of a grainer. Piggy-back trailers were after that, if you could find a place between the wheels. Then second or third deck of empty auto carriers.

But don't be afraid to check the doors of vehicles on full auto carriers. Every once a while you'll find one unlocked. But if you do, leave it as clean as you found it. If you have to, and feel brave, go ahead and ride on the back engine.

Avoid grabbing shaky parts of a train car, like rusty handles or anything that might break under your weight. Keep three points of contact when standing— two legs and a handhold or, when moving, two handholds and one leg. Lie as low as possible in case of an emergency stop.

Bridges, tunnels, traffic lights, train lights and trains from other directions are danger. Especially tunnels. Never ride with your head above a train car at night. You'll never see what hit you.

Never, absolutely never, jump on or off a moving train if it is going faster than you can run.

Stone tried to blink away the memory of the Calgary train yard. Never hurt to have a repeat of that advice.

If you have to leave a train in motion—like if the bulls are about to catch you—get to the lowest footrest, face in the direction of the train's movement and land running.

Take plenty of water.

Dress in layers.

Take trail mix.

Use the walkie-talkie to listen for yard bulls.

Stone repeated all that advice like a mantra.

Sure, he was alone now. But he was confident he could ride the rails. After all, Joseph had taught him all of those things during the hundreds upon hundreds upon hundreds of kilometers of travel.

Except his destination wasn't Vancouver. Not yet. No reason to go back, but no reason to run. He'd finally found something on the Internet. Dude he'd hit with the van had walked away, told the cops the crash was his fault. Got a ticket for careless driving. Probably didn't want them looking too closely into his life.

What was sending Stone eastward was the itch to move, to keep moving. He had time before school started. He'd checked in with Violet and renegotiated a long-term agreement. Turned out that Violet and his mom got along just fine.

Stone was curious to see how the flat, open land east of Winnipeg suddenly turned into the rock and trees and small black lakes that Joseph had described. He wanted to see the farmlands of southern Ontario and the outline of huge ships cruising the St. Lawrence. He wanted to smell the ocean at Halifax. The Pacific had been on his doorstep his entire life, but he hadn't even bothered to go to the beach. Hadn't wanted to. Now he was on his way across Canada to seek out the salt waters of the Atlantic. Ironic, right?

Joseph had told him yard bulls in Winnipeg were aggressive. What you did was wait on the other side of the Assiniboine River. Tracks leaving downtown curved to the east. Trains didn't start picking up speed until well across the river. You found a hole in a fence, caught the train before it could get much past walking speed.

So Stone headed for the river.

Chapter Twenty-Four

Perfect. Ten cars down from the engine was a boxcar. Much farther down, and the train might have been going too fast. This was worth the five hours of waiting.

Stone left the bush that had screened him from the tracks and started to jog. His backpack flopped against his back. This irritated him. He should have made sure it was cinched tight. Now he'd have to worry about whether it would throw his balance off as he made a jump for the train.

A quick vision of the kid lying on the gravel in Calgary, face tight in agony, flashed through Stone's mind. He told himself to ignore it.

He focused on the spinning wheel bolts.

If you can see them individually, it's slow enough to make the leap.

Joseph's voice in his head. Stone expected to hear that a lot over the next thousands of kilometers to the Atlantic coast and back again to the Pacific. Maybe Joseph wouldn't be with him, but remembering Joseph would be enough.

None of the bolts had begun to blur in a circle.

He timed his jump and found a hand-rail on the side of the boxcar. He swung his legs up and onto the lowest footrest.

There!

He was on.

What a rush.

Both hands on the rail now until he was sure of his balance. Then into the shade of the boxcar.

Looking back, he saw a large hand grab the same handrail.

Large. As in Joseph large.

Joseph swung into the boxcar.

Eyes met. Subtle nods rather than jumping into each other's arms like it was some dumb movie and the big reunion with sweeping music or anything.

Joseph didn't like talk, so Stone kept his mouth shut. Plenty of things Stone knew now that he hadn't known earlier. On the way to the train yard, he'd stopped at a library.

What he knew about Joseph Nelson had been enough to make some guesses as he hit the Internet. Joseph knew the cop system. Joseph knew paramedics. Joseph was calm in an emergency. Joseph had easily acquired Stone's father's address in Winnipeg.

It all added up to some kind of ex-cop. Someone who could make a phone call and call in a favor. Someone who had access to national network databases.

Hadn't taken much of a search to discover that Joseph Nelson had once been a CN cop himself. Hadn't taken much of a search to learn about a crossing accident—freight train versus a minivan. Kids in the fire that followed, and Joseph ignoring the flames to drag them out. Stone could picture the crushed metal, could hear the screaming, could see Joseph pulling them free, then collapsing in agony.

Not even that much of a guess to figure out how life after that had unfolded for Joseph. Stone remembered the sarcastic comment Joseph had made about saving up for a house so he could live in one place for a change and watch everyone in the neighborhood try to avoid looking at his face.

Back in Kamloops, Joseph hadn't been worried about yard bulls. He'd only wanted to make it look that way to Stone.

It's him, one of the voices behind the flashlight had said. *Legend.*

A former CN cop who had made a choice to ride the rails and keep doing what good cops did. Because what else was he going to do?

Stone thought about all of this as he stared into Joseph's face. His knowledge of Joseph's past and his guess at Joseph's reason for riding the rails weren't things he'd ever bring up. If Joseph wanted to tell Stone about it, that was okay. Stone was learning how to listen. .

More silence. The nobody's-talking kind of silence. Nothing else was silent, not in a behemoth gaining nearly unstoppable speed. Train noise wasn't at maximum yet, but soon enough conversation could only take place at yell volume. Which probably meant there was going to be no conversation for a while.

Stone was good with that. He settled back to enjoy the moving countryside.

Eventually Joseph spoke.

"Next time, Max," he said, "make sure the backpack is tight. Sloppy the way it bounced when you ran. Very sloppy."

"You're crap at hiding, you know," Stone answered. "Saw you just down the tracks, watching me like you thought I didn't know you were there."

"Surprised you didn't come over and try to talk my ears off."

"Ear," Stone said. "You only have one."

Joseph rubbed the melted side of his head, the ear stub as disfigured as the other scarred tissue. "Surprised you didn't come over and try to talk my ear off."

"Thought if you wanted to ride alone, I wasn't going to force myself on you for the trip. Didn't need you anyway."

"I *was* going to let you travel alone," Joseph said. "But then I saw how loose that backpack was. Clearly, you still need babysitting." Joseph paused. "Actually, that's not true. I wasn't going to let you travel alone. But I wanted to see how you'd handle it by yourself before I jumped on board. I feel an obligation to get you back to Vancouver, you know. Good grades and all, and a business you want to own someday, Max. Don't lose sight of that."

It occurred to Stone that if Joseph actually went with him all the way back to East Hastings, maybe Stone would see about getting him to stay. Lots of broken people in East Hastings. Nobody would feel sorry for him there. And it would be nice to have the company. Plus Van Dudes wouldn't mess with Stone if Joseph was there. Not the time to mention that though.

"Halifax first. But we need to get things figured out," Stone said. He shifted his backpack to make himself comfortable.

"Like what?"

"I think you should allow me more than one question a day."

"Why?"

"It's hard work, figuring out a way to get answers without asking a question."

"Like saying you want more than one question a day instead of asking for more than one question a day?"

"See. It's easier for you. You get to ask."

"Okay. Two questions each day. Anything else?"

"Yes. Can you *please* stop calling me Max? And I don't care if that counts as my first question today."

"I'll consider it," Joseph said, shifting his own backpack and settling in for the ride. "Give me a good reason."

"We're riding the rails from here to Halifax, and then back across Canada to Vancouver." Stone paused for effect. "If you're going to be my sidekick for that kind of distance, I should get to choose what you call me."

"Sidekick? I'm your sidekick?"

Stone grinned. "Unless you prefer minion."

Joseph's mouth opened and out came a sound Stone had never heard from Joseph before.

Laughter.

Sigmund Brouwer has written dozens of books for both children and adults, including *Devil's Pass*, *Tin Soldier* and *Barracuda* from the Orca Seven series. Sigmund and his family live half the year in Nashville, Tennessee, and half the year in Red Deer, Alberta. He also visits schools to talk about Rock and Roll Literacy. For more information, visit www.sigmundbrouwer.com.